For Rosemary J. — her book ✳ M. W.

For Ellen ✳ S. F-D.

First U.S. edition 2003

Library of Congress Cataloging-in-Publication Data

Waddell, Martin.
Snow bears / Martin Waddell ; illustrated by Sarah Fox-Davies.
p.   cm.
Summary: When three little bears play in the snow, they pretend to be
"snow bears" and their mother goes along with the game.
ISBN 0-7636-1906-X
[1. Mother and child—Fiction. 2. Bears—Fiction. 3. Play—Fiction.
4. Snow—Fiction.] I. Fox-Davies, Sarah, ill. II. Title.
PZ7.W1137 Sn 2002
[E]—dc21   2001058258

2 4 6 8 10 9 7 5 3

Printed in Italy

This book was typeset in Veronan.
The illustrations were done in watercolor and pencil.

Candlewick Press
2067 Massachusetts Avenue
Cambridge, Massachusetts 02140

visit us at www.candlewick.com

Snow Bears

Martin Waddell

illustrated by Sarah Fox-Davies

CANDLEWICK PRESS
CAMBRIDGE, MASSACHUSETTS

Mommy Bear came out to play with her
baby bears. They were all covered with snow.
"You look like snow bears," Mommy Bear said.
"That's what we are," said the three baby bears.
"We are snow bears!"
And that's how their snow bear game began.
"But where are *my* baby bears?" Mommy Bear asked.

"I don't know where we are," said the biggest snow bear.

"I haven't seen us," said the middle-sized snow bear.

"We aren't here, Mommy Bear," said the smallest snow bear.

"Then who can I play with?" sighed Mommy Bear.

"We'll play with you, Mommy Bear," said the snow bears.
"What games will we play?" asked Mommy Bear.
"Let's slide," said the biggest
snow bear.

They slid down the slope and . . .

BOOOOOOOOOOOM!

The smallest snow bear got snow on her nose.
"My bears would like playing that game,"
Mommy Bear said. "Are you sure you haven't
seen *my* baby bears?"

"I don't know where
we are," said the
biggest snow bear.

"I haven't seen us,"
said the middle-sized
snow bear.

"We aren't here,
Mommy Bear," said
the smallest snow bear.

"What will we play next?" Mommy Bear asked.
"We snowball you, and
you snowball us,"
said the middle-sized
snow bear.

SPLOT

SPLOT

SPLOT

SPLOT!

The smallest snow bear
couldn't throw very well.
Her paws were as cold
as her nose.

"Three against one isn't fair!" Mommy Bear said.
"I wonder where *my* baby bears can be?"
"I don't know where we are," said the biggest snow bear.
"I haven't seen us," said the middle-sized snow bear.
"We aren't here, Mommy Bear," said the
smallest snow bear.

"It's your turn to pick the next game,"
Mommy Bear said to the smallest snow bear.
"I'm too cold to play games," said the smallest
snow bear. "I want to go home."

"Hot toast by the fire will soon warm you up,"
Mommy Bear said. "My baby bears like hot toast."
"So do we," said the snow bears.

Mommy Bear carried the smallest snow bear
in her arms as they all went back to the
warmth of the house.

DRIP . . .

"Something's happening to us,"
said the biggest snow bear.

DRIP . . . DRIP . . .

"We're starting to drip,"
said the middle-sized
snow bear.

DRIP . . . DRIP . . . DRIP!

"We're melting away," said
the smallest snow bear.

Mommy Bear came back with the toast.
She saw her three baby bears by the
fire where the snow bears had been.
"My baby bears!" Mommy Bear said.
"Yes! It's us!" said the three baby bears.
"But where are the snow bears I left
by the fire?" Mommy Bear asked.

"There weren't any snow bears," said the biggest baby bear.

"We were playing tricks," said the middle-sized baby bear.

"It was us all the time, Mommy Bear," said the smallest baby bear.

"But I made this toast for the snow bears!" Mommy Bear said.

"We'll eat the toast!" said the three baby bears.

Then they all had hot toast by the fire,
Mommy Bear and her three baby bears.